ALICE
IN WONDERLAND

TREASURY OF ILLUSTRATED CLASSICS™

ALICE
IN WONDERLAND

by
Lewis Carroll

**Abridged, adapted,
and illustrated**

by

quadrum■
Quadrum Solutions, India

Modern Publishing
A Division of Unisystems, Inc.
New York, New York 10022

Series UPC: 38150

Cover art by Michele Nidenoff

Contents

Chapter 1
Down the Rabbit Hole — 9

Chapter 2
The Pool of Tears — 25

Chapter 3
A Caucus Race and
a Long Tale — 39

Chapter 4
The Rabbit Sends
in a Little Bill — 51

Chapter 5
Advice from a Caterpillar — 63

Chapter 6
Pig and Pepper — 71

Chapter 7
A Mad Tea Party — 83

Chapter 8
The Queen's Croquet Ground — 95

Chapter 9
The Mock Turtle's Story — 117

Chapter 10
The Lobster Quadrille — 133

Chapter 11
 Who Stole the Tarts? 151
Chapter 12
 Alice's Evidence 171

About the Author 189

Chapter 1

Down the Rabbit Hole

One sunny afternoon, Alice was in her garden, listening to her sister reading. Once or twice she had peeped into the book, but it had no pictures or conversations in it. "What is the use of a book," thought Alice, "without pictures or conversations?"

Alice soon fell asleep, but woke up sometime later upon hearing a noise. She looked around for her sister, but found herself alone. Suddenly, a White Rabbit with pink eyes ran by her. He was dressed in a blue suit and was carrying a large pocket watch. He kept saying to himself, "Oh dear, oh dear! I shall be too late!"

"I wonder why he is in such a hurry?" thought Alice.

She jumped up when she saw

the Rabbit take the watch out of his waistcoat pocket. Out of curiosity, she followed him out of the garden and into the woods, for she realized just then that never had she seen a rabbit wearing a waistcoat, nor had she seen a rabbit carrying a pocket watch!

She followed him until he disappeared down a hole near a big tree. Before she could stop herself, she found that she too had entered the rabbit hole. As she crawled on her knees she said to herself, "It is so dark in here! Where on earth did the Rabbit disappear to?"

The rabbit hole went straight on like a tunnel and then dipped down so suddenly that Alice had no time to finish off her thought before she found herself falling

down what seemed to be a very
deep well!

"Aaaaahhhhh!!!" screamed
Alice as she fell deeper into the

hole. She fell for what seemed like a very long time. Either the well was very deep, or she fell very slowly, for she had plenty of time as she went down to look about her and wonder what was going to happen next.

First, she tried to look down and make out where she was going, but it was too dark to see anything. Then she looked at the sides of the well and noticed that they were filled with cupboards and bookshelves; here and there she saw maps and pictures hung upon pegs.

Alice took down a jar from one of the shelves as she passed; it was labeled "Orange Marmalade," but to her great disappointment, it was empty. She did not want

to drop the jar for fear of killing somebody, so she managed to put it into one of the cupboards as she fell past it.

Would the fall ever end? She started wishing her cat Dinah was with her. Suddenly, she landed on a pile of dry leaves. She got up

and dusted the leaves off her. She then looked up and saw the White Rabbit running down a narrow corridor.

She ran after it and could hear him say, "Oh dear! Oh

my! I'm late! I'm late!" She called out to him, "Mr. Rabbit! Please wait!" When Alice turned around the corner, the White Rabbit had disappeared!

She found herself in a long, low hall, which was lit up by a row of lamps hanging from the roof. She saw a number of doors before her. She tried all of them and found that they were all locked. She sadly walked from one end to another, wondering, "How am I to get out of here?"

She saw a glass table with nothing but a tiny, golden key on it. She looked around to see if the key would open the doors, but the locks were too big! Suddenly, she noticed a small curtain

that she hadn't seen before, covering a very tiny door. She tried the golden key and to her delight found that the key opened the tiny door!

Alice opened the door and found that it led into a small passage. She knelt down and looked along the passage into the most beautiful garden she had ever seen, with bright flower beds and cool fountains. "Oh," said Alice, "How I wish I were small enough to fit through this door. I would love to go into that garden."

She looked around to see if she could find another key, and found a little bottle on the glass table with a note around it that

said "DRINK ME" in beautifully painted letters. She tasted the liquid in the bottle and finding it very nice, she very soon finished it off.

The moment she finished the last drop, she became tiny! She was now only ten inches high. To her delight, she was small enough to go through the tiny door! She ran to the door and tried to open it, only to see that it was locked.

Alice had forgotten the golden key on the glass table, which was as big as a mountain now! She tried to climb to the top, but kept slipping. After trying many times, Alice sat down and started to cry.

When she stopped crying, she saw a tiny glass box under the

table with the words "EAT ME" beautifully marked out in currants. Wiping her tears, Alice took a bite of the cake that was inside the box.

She thought to herself, "If by eating this, I grow bigger, I can get the key to the door. If I grow smaller, I can crawl under the door

and get to the other side. I will get to that garden no matter what!"

Chapter 2

The Pool
of Tears

Alice had a small piece of the cake, and checked if she had grown in size. To her disappointment, she hadn't grown even an inch. Shrugging her shoulders, she finished off the cake. After that, she suddenly grew!

"Curiouser and curiouser!" cried Alice. She was so surprised that for a moment, she forgot how to speak English properly. "Now I'm opening up like a telescope. And a rather large one!" She looked down at her feet only to see that she had grown so tall, she couldn't even see them. "Good-bye, feet! I wonder who will put on your shoes and stockings for you," she called.

Just then, the top of her head struck the roof of the hall. She was at least nine feet tall! She picked up the golden key and turned to the door. But poor Alice was so huge that going through the door was impossible. She sat down and began to cry. Huge tears dropped from her eyes. She cried so much that soon there was a

pool of tears around her, spreading into the hall.

At that moment, she heard the patter of feet. She quickly dried her eyes and looked up to see who was coming. It was the White Rabbit, splendidly dressed, with kid gloves in one hand and a large fan in the other. He kept saying to himself, "Oh dear! The duchess! Won't she be upset if I keep her waiting?"

As he neared Alice, she called out, "If you please, sir . . ." To her surprise, he jumped in fright on seeing her. He dropped the fan and the gloves and ran into the darkness as fast as he could.

Alice picked up the fan and

started fanning herself, all the while muttering, "Dear me! Everything is so odd today! Yesterday things went on just as usual. I wonder if I've changed through the night. Was I the same person when I got up this morning? If not, then who am I? Ah, that's the great puzzle!"

As she said this, she looked

down and saw that she had put on one of the gloves while talking. "Now how could I have done that unless I'm getting smaller?" she wondered. She stood up and measured herself. She realized she was two feet tall and shrinking rapidly. It was because of the fan. The more she fanned herself, the more she shrunk! She quickly dropped the fan.

"That was a narrow escape! Now for the garden." She ran back to the door, happy to see she was the right size but sad to see that the key was on the glass table as before. "Things are worse than ever," said Alice, "for I was never this small."

Just then, her foot slipped and

she fell in the salt water. At first she thought she had fallen into the sea, but then she realized it was the pool of tears that she had made crying. She heard someone splashing her way. She swam nearer to make out what it was.

At first she thought it must be

a walrus or hippopotamus, but then she remembered how small she was now, and she soon realized that it was only a mouse that had slipped in the salt water like herself.

"Would it be any use now," said Alice, "to speak to this mouse? Everything here is so strange, it is quite likely that he will talk. There's no harm trying." She

began, "Oh, mouse! Do you know the way out of this pool? I am very tired of swimming about here. Oh, Mouse!"

The mouse looked at her inquisitively but said nothing. "Perhaps he doesn't understand English. Maybe he's a French mouse!" she thought. So she asked in French, *"Où est mon chat?"* which in English meant "Where is my cat?"

Suddenly the mouse leaped out of the water and shook with fright.

"Oh, I beg your pardon!" cried Alice. "I quite forgot that you don't like cats." "Not like cats!" shrieked the mouse. "Would you like cats if you were me?"

"Well, perhaps not," said Alice in a soothing tone. "But don't be angry about it. You'd start liking cats after meeting Dinah, my cat. She is such a darling." She stopped when she saw the mouse becoming angry. "Oh, I beg your pardon! We won't talk about Dinah anymore, if you'd rather not."

"Well, indeed," cried the mouse, who was trembling down to the end of his tail. "As if

I would talk about such a subject. Our family has always hated cats—nasty, low, vulgar things! Don't let me hear the name again!"

"I won't indeed," promised Alice, eager to change the topic. "Are you . . . are . . . you . . . fond . . . of . . . of . . . dogs? . . . Oh, dear! I've offended you again!"

But the mouse was swimming away as fast as he could, splashing water everywhere. She called out to it softly, "Mouse dear, do come back, we won't talk about cats or dogs if you don't like them." On hearing this, the mouse turned around and slowly swam back, his face quite pale. He said in a trembling voice, "Let us get to the shore. I will tell you the story of my life. Then you'll understand why I hate cats and dogs."

Alice looked around her and saw that the pool was now crowded with animals and birds. There was a duck, a dodo, which was a big, clumsy bird that couldn't fly, an eaglet, a brilliantly colored parrot called a lory, and several other curious creatures. Alice led the way, and the whole party swam to shore.

Chapter 3

A Caucus Race and a Long Tale

It was indeed a strange group that came to shore, birds with wet and ruffled feathers, animals with their fur clinging to them, all dripping wet, angry, and uncomfortable. They all had a talk

about how to get dry. After a while, Alice felt quite at ease with them, like she'd known them all her life. At last, the mouse, who seemed to be the figure of authority amongst them, called out, "Sit down, all of you, and listen to me. I'll soon

make you dry enough."

They all sat down at once in a large circle, with the mouse in the middle. "Ahem," said the mouse with an important air. "Are you all ready?" He told them a dull story of William the Conqueror that almost put them to sleep.

"Ugh," said the dodo with a shiver.

"I beg your pardon," replied the mouse, frowning but trying to be polite. "Did you say something?"

"I'm sorry, but your story has not dried us one bit! We are still soaking wet, the lot of us," explained the poor, bored dodo. "I think the best way for us to dry ourselves is to have a caucus race."

"What is a caucus race?" asked Alice.

"Why," said the dodo, "the best way to explain it is to do it."

He marked a circular race-course and made everyone take positions around it. No one ever called out, "One, two, three, go!"

but all the creatures began running and stopping whenever they felt like it. However, after running for half an hour, everyone was dry.

The dodo suddenly called out, "The race is over!" and everyone stopped, holding their sides and panting. "But who won?" they asked. This question the dodo could not answer. He sat for a long time with one finger pressed upon his forehead, thinking hard.

After thinking for a long time, he answered, "Everybody's won! All must have prizes."

"But who's to give the prizes?" everyone asked.

"Why, she of course!" said the dodo, pointing to Alice.

They all crowded around her, asking for their prize. Quite confused, she reached into her pocket and pulled out a packet of comfits, which thankfully hadn't gotten soaked. She handed one each to everyone—fortunately there was just about enough.

"But she must have a prize herself, you know," said the mouse.

"Of course," the dodo replied very gravely. "What else have you got in your pocket?" he went on, turning to Alice.

"Only a thimble," said Alice sadly. "Give it to me," said the dodo.

Then they all crowded around

her once more, while the dodo presented the thimble, saying, "We would like you to accept this elegant thimble." When he had finished this short speech, they all cheered.

Alice thought the whole thing was very silly, but they all looked so grave that she did not dare to laugh. As she could not think of anything to say, she simply bowed and took the thimble, looking as serious as she could.

After the prize distribution, she walked up to the mouse and asked him to tell her his life story— the reason he hated "C and D."

"Mine is a long and sad tale," sighed the mouse.

Alice looked down at the

mouse's tail, "Yes, it is a long tail, but why do you call it sad?" She thought he was speaking of his tail.

"You are not listening to me," said the mouse, frowning at Alice. "What are you thinking of?"

"Oh, forgive me," said Alice. "You got to the fifth bend, I think."

"You insult me by talking such nonsense," said the mouse angrily, and walked away.

"Please come back!" cried Alice to him. But the mouse just shook his head and angrily walked away.

"Oh, I wish I had my cat Dinah here," said Alice, "She'd soon fetch

him back!"

"And who is Dinah, if I might dare to ask the question?" said the lory.

Alice replied eagerly, for she was always ready to talk about her pet. "Dinah's our cat. And she's such an expert for catching mice! And oh, I wish you could see her after the birds! Why, she'll eat a little bird as soon as she sees it!" On hearing this, all the other creatures ran away, leaving Alice all alone.

"I wish I hadn't mentioned poor Dinah. Nobody seems to like her here, and I think she's the best cat in the whole world!" Poor Alice started crying once more. Just then she heard the patter of feet. She stopped crying and eagerly looked up.

Chapter 4

The Rabbit Sends in a Little Bill

It was the White Rabbit! He was walking back and forth, looking anxiously around him, as if he had lost something. He kept saying to himself, "The duchess! The duchess! Oh, my dear paws! Oh, my fur and whiskers!

She'll have me executed, that's for sure! Where could I have dropped them?"

Alice guessed that he was looking for his fan and white kid gloves, so she happily began looking for them. But they were nowhere to be found. Everything had vanished—the glass table, the

little bottle, everything!

Soon, the Rabbit noticed Alice. He called out to her angrily, "Why, Mary Ann! What are you doing out here? Run inside and fetch me my gloves. Quick!" As Alice ran off, she thought to herself, "He mistook me for his housemaid! He'll be surprised to find out who I really am!"

She came upon a neat, little house with a brass nameplate engraved with "W. Rabbit." She hurried upstairs, fearing that she would run into the real Mary Ann. She entered a tidy room and soon found a fan and three pairs of gloves on a table by the window. She picked up a pair and was about to leave the room, when she spotted a glass

MR. W.
RABBIT

bottle near a mirror.

She opened it and thought, "I know something interesting is sure to happen whenever I eat or drink anything; so I'll just see what this bottle does. I do hope when I drink this, it will make me grow again. I'm so tired of being tiny!"

She had hardly finished off

half the bottle when she found the top of her head touching the ceiling! She crouched, lest she bang her head. "That's enough. I don't want to grow anymore." But she went on growing and growing until soon, she was so big that she had to stick one arm out the window and one foot up the chimney! "Oh, dear," she said, "what will become of me now?"

Luckily for Alice, the little magic bottle had now had its

full effect, and she grew no larger. Still, it was very uncomfortable, and there seemed to be no chance of her ever getting out of the room again.

Just then she heard a voice outside, "Mary Ann! Fetch me my gloves this instant!" She heard the Rabbit coming up the stairs. He tried to open the door, but couldn't, as Alice's elbow was pressed against it. She heard him mutter angrily, "I'll go around and get in through the window."

"Oh no, you won't," thought Alice. She waited until she heard the Rabbit outside the window. Then she made a grab for him. She didn't catch him, but she heard a cry, a fall, and a crash of broken glass. She soon heard the Rabbit calling out angrily for someone called Pat. He was asking Pat to help him get the monster out of his house.

Alice waited until she heard scampering on the wall outside. Again, she tried to grab. This time she heard two shrieks and more sounds of glass breaking. "I wonder what they'll do next. As for pulling me out, I wish they could!"

She soon heard the rumbling of a cart and many voices talking at once. Alice stuck her foot as much as she could into the chimney until she heard an animal making its way downward. She then gave it a nice kick.

"There goes Bill!" she heard everyone cry. Then the Rabbit shouted, "Catch him by the hedge!" There were other voices babbling away asking Bill if he was all right. At last came a weak, squeaking voice that Alice knew must be Bill's. "I'm better now. But all I know is that something came up at me like a Jack-in-the-Box, and up I go like a sky rocket!"

Alice heard a lot of moving around. She heard the Rabbit say, "A barrowful will do."

"A barrowful of what?" thought Alice. In reply, a shower of pebbles came right through the window on her face. Alice noticed with surprise that the pebbles, on touching the floor, turned into little cakes. She

soon thought that eating one of these cakes would definitely change her size. She picked up a cake and ate it, delighted to find out that she was shrinking immediately.

As soon as she was small enough to get through the door, she ran out of the house and found quite a crowd of little animals and birds waiting outside. They all made a rush at Alice the moment she appeared; but she ran off as fast as she could, into the woods.

"The first thing I've got to do," she said, "is to get back to the right size. The second thing is to find that lovely garden. Yes, I think that's a good plan."

It sounded like an excellent plan, but she had no idea how to go about it. While she was peering about anxiously among the trees, a little sharp bark just over her head made her look up in a great hurry.

An enormous puppy was looking down at her with large, round eyes and feebly stretching out one paw, trying to touch her.

"Poor little thing!" said Alice, and she tried hard to whistle to

it, even though she was terribly
frightened the whole time that it
might be hungry and might eat her
up. She picked up a little stick
and held it out to the puppy.
The puppy jumped into the air
with a yelp of delight and rushed
at the stick. This seemed to Alice
a good opportunity for making
her escape. So she set off at
once, and ran till she was quite

tired and out of breath, and till the puppy's bark sounded faint in the distance.

She looked around her but didn't see anything worth eating or drinking. She saw a rather large mushroom with a caterpillar sitting on it. He was sitting with his arms folded, quietly smoking a hookah. He didn't seem interested in her, or anything else around him.

Chapter 5

Advice from a Caterpillar

The caterpillar finally took the hookah out of his mouth and asked Alice in a sleepy voice, "Who are you?"

"I hardly know, sir," replied Alice. "I knew who I was when

I woke up this morning, but I've changed so many times since then."

"Explain yourself," said the caterpillar.

"I can't explain myself, I'm afraid, because I'm not myself. Changing sizes so many times in a day can be confusing!" said Alice. "I think you should tell me who you are, first."

The caterpillar seemed to be unpleasant and not able to come up with a good answer, so she turned and started walking away. "Come back!" called the caterpillar. "I have something important to tell you."

When Alice returned to him, he told her not to get angry. "Is that all?" she asked, trying to control her anger.

The caterpillar shook his head. "So you think you've changed, have you?"

"I'm afraid I have, sir," said Alice.

"What size do you want to be?" asked the caterpillar.

"Oh, I'm not particular to any size," Alice replied hastily. "I'm just so tired of changing often, you know. I would like, though, to be a little taller than you. Three inches is such an awful height!"

"I beg your pardon! Three inches is a very good height to be!" said the caterpillar angrily, and rose to his full three inches. He got off the mushroom and crawled into the grass. He could be heard saying, "One side will make you grow taller, the other side will make you grow shorter."

As Alice thought to herself, "One side of what?" the caterpillar replied as if she had spoken aloud. "The mushroom," he said, and disappeared. Alice looked at the mushroom, trying to understand which side

did what.

Finally, she broke off a bit of the mushroom from either side. She slowly took a bite of the piece in her right hand. The next moment, her chin struck her foot in a violent blow. Her jawline was pressed so closely to her foot that she was hardly able to open her mouth. She, however, managed to take a bite from the piece in her left hand. But she was soon dismayed to find out that she couldn't see her body anywhere below the neck. She realized that her neck had grown so much, she looked like a serpent, with her head stuck above the trees.

Suddenly, a pigeon attacked her, beating her violently with its wings. "Serpent! Serpent!" cried the pigeon.

"I'm not a serpent!" cried Alice. "Leave me alone!"

"I've tried the roots of trees, the riverbanks, even hedges! But those serpents are always after me! I've been on the lookout for them. I haven't slept in weeks," said the distressed bird.

"I'm so sorry for your condition. But I'm not a serpent. I— I'm—I'm just a little girl!" said Alice.

"So what does it matter if you are a girl? You're still looking for eggs!" said the pigeon angrily.

"It matters to me," replied Alice. "I'm not looking for eggs, and if I was, I wouldn't be after yours. I hate having them raw."

"Well, off with you, then!" the bird cried and settled in its nest.

Alice tried to snake her neck

down without entangling herself. She remembered that she still held the mushroom pieces in her hand. She started nibbling, carefully, one piece, then the other, until she was back to her usual height.

It felt strange getting back to her normal height. "There. That's done. Now, how do I get to the garden?" She soon saw a house only four feet tall. She knew that she would scare those living there, so she brought herself to a height where she could enter the house.

Chapter 6

Pig and Pepper

Alice spent a minute looking at the house. Just then she saw a footman, elegantly dressed, running to the front door. His face looked like that of a fish. He knocked loudly until the door was opened by another footman whose face looked like a frog's. The

Fish-Footman began by producing from under his arm a great letter, and this he handed over to the Frog-Footman.

"For the duchess. An invitation from the queen to play croquet." Then they bowed down to each other and their curls got entangled.

Alice laughed so much at this that she had to run back into the wood for fear of them hearing her. When she next peeped out, the Fish-Footman was gone, and the Frog-Footman was sitting on the ground near the door, staring stupidly up into the sky.

Alice went up and timidly knocked on the door, while the Frog-Footman sat outside. "There is no reason to knock. Firstly, because I am outside as well, and secondly, they are making far too much noise inside to hear you," said the footman to Alice.

At that moment, the door of the house opened, and a large plate came skimming out, straight at the footman's head. It just grazed his nose, and broke to pieces against one of the trees behind him.

Alice entered the house, which led to a large kitchen full of smoke. She saw the duchess sitting on a three-legged stool, nursing a baby, while the cook was bent over a cauldron, possibly filled with

soup.

"There is far too much pepper in the soup, I'm quite sure," said Alice, sneezing. The duchess sneezed occasionally; the baby sneezed and howled at the same time. The only two people who weren't sneezing were the cook and a large cat, which was grinning from ear to ear.

"Why is your cat grinning like that?" Alice asked the duchess. "He's a Cheshire Cat, that's why."

"I didn't know Cheshire Cats grinned. I didn't know cats could grin at all!" said Alice.

Just then the cook took the cauldron off the fire and started throwing everything within her reach at the duchess. Vessels and

iron pans hit her, and the baby was howling so much in the first place that it was difficult to say if it got hurt or not.

"Oh, please watch what you are doing!" cried Alice angrily.

"Here, you may nurse the baby, if you like," said the duchess. "I must get ready to go play croquet with the queen." She flung the baby at Alice, who caught it with some difficulty. Then, the duchess hurried out of the room. The cook threw a frying pan after her as she went out, but it just missed her.

"If I don't take the baby away now, they will surely kill it in a day or two!" thought Alice. The baby grunted in reply. "If you turn into a

pig, I will have nothing more to do with you," said Alice to the baby, who grunted again.

Alice looked very anxiously into its face to see what the matter with it was. There was no doubt that it had a VERY turned-up nose, much more like a snout than a real nose. Also, its eyes were getting extremely small for a baby.

Altogether, Alice did not like the look of the thing at all. "But perhaps it is only sobbing," she thought, and looked into its eyes again, to see if there were any tears. Then it grunted again so violently that she looked down into its face with some alarm. This time, there was no mistake about it: It was a pig, and she felt that it would be quite absurd for her to carry it further. She let the creature down and saw it trotting off into the woods.

She saw the Cheshire Cat grinning down at her. She asked

the cat which way she should go.

"In that direction lives the Mad Hatter," replied the Cat. "In the other, lives the March Hare. I must tell you that they are both mad."

"Oh, but I don't want to go among mad people!" said Alice.

"That cannot be helped. We are all mad here," said the Cheshire Cat, and smiled.

"Are you playing croquet with the queen today?"

"I should very much like to," replied Alice, "but I haven't been invited."

"I will see you there." Saying this, the Cheshire Cat disappeared.

Alice soon saw the house of the March Hare. The chimneys were shaped like ears, and the roof was thatched with fur. It was so large a house that she did not like to go nearer till she had nibbled some more of the left-hand bit of mushroom, and was then about two feet high.

Chapter 7

A Mad Tea Party

There was a large table in the backyard. The Mad Hatter and the March Hare were enjoying their tea, a dormouse fast asleep between them. The other two were using it as a cushion, resting their elbows on it, and talking over its head.

The table was a large one, but the three were all crowded together at one corner of it.

"No room! No room!" they cried out when they saw Alice toward them.

"There's PLENTY of room!" said Alice indignantly, and she sat down in a large armchair at one end of the table.

"Have some wine," the March Hare said in an encouraging tone. Alice looked all around the table, but there was nothing on it but tea. "I don't see any wine," she remarked.

"There isn't any," said the March Hare.

"Then it wasn't very nice of you to offer it," said Alice angrily.

"It wasn't very nice of you to sit down without being invited," said the March Hare.

"Your hair needs cutting," said the Hatter. He had been looking at Alice for some time with great curiosity, and this was his first speech.

"You should learn not to make personal remarks," Alice said sternly. "It's very rude."

The Hatter opened his eyes very wide on hearing this, but all he said was, "Why is a raven like a writing desk?"

"I think I can guess that," said Alice out loud.

"You mean you can find the answer to it?"

"Yes."

"Then say what you mean," the March Hare went on.

"I do," Alice hastily replied. "At least, I mean what I say—that's the same thing, you know."

"It is the same thing with you," said the Hatter, and he poured a little hot tea on the dormouse's nose. The dormouse shook its head impatiently and said, without opening its eyes, "Of course, of course, just what I was going to remark myself."

The party sat silent for a minute while Alice thought over all she could remember about ravens and writing desks, which wasn't much.

The Hatter was the first to break the silence. "What day of the month is it?" he asked, turning to Alice. He had taken his watch out of his pocket and was looking at it uneasily, shaking it every now and then and holding it to his ear.

Alice thought for a while and then said, "The fourth."

"Two days wrong!" The Hatter sighed. "I told you butter wouldn't suit the works!' he added, looking angrily at the March Hare.

"It was the best butter," the

March Hare meekly replied.

"Yes, but some crumbs must have got in as well," the Hatter grumbled. "You shouldn't have put it in with the breadknife."

The March Hare took the watch and looked at it gloomily. Then he dipped it into his cup of tea and looked at it again. But he could think of nothing better to say than his first remark: "It was the best butter, you know."

Alice had been looking over his shoulder with some curiosity. "What a funny watch!" she remarked. "It tells the day of the month, and doesn't tell what o'clock it is!"

"Have you guessed the riddle yet?" the Mad Hatter asked, turning to Alice again. "No, I give it up,"

Alice replied. "What's the answer?"

"I haven't the slightest idea," said the Mad Hatter.

"Nor I," said the March Hare.

"You must do something better with your time rather than waste it on asking riddles with no answer," said Alice with a sigh.

"Suppose we change the subject," the March Hare interrupted, yawning. "I'm getting tired of this. I vote the young lady tells us a story."

"I'm afraid I don't know one," said Alice, rather alarmed at the proposal.

"Then the dormouse shall!" they both cried. "Wake up, Dormouse!" And they pinched it on both sides at once.

"Tell us a story!" said the March Hare.

"Yes, please do!" pleaded Alice.

"And be quick about it," added the Hatter, "or you'll be asleep again before it's done." Before the dormouse could begin his story, the March Hare interrupted him. "Take some more tea," the March Hare said to Alice, very earnestly.

"I've had nothing yet," Alice replied in an offended tone, "so I can't take more."

"You mean you can't take less," said the Hatter. "It's very easy to take more than nothing."

"I want a clean cup," interrupted the Hatter. "Let's all move one place on." He moved on as he spoke, and the dormouse followed him. The March Hare moved into the dormouse's place, and Alice rather unwillingly took the place of the March Hare. The Hatter was the only one who got any advantage from the change. Alice was a good deal worse off than before, as the March Hare had just upset the milkjug into his plate.

At this, Alice got up and walked off. The dormouse fell asleep instantly, and neither of the others took the least notice of

her going, though she looked back once or twice. As she was walking away, she saw them trying to put the dormouse into the teapot.

"That was the stupidest tea party I've ever been to in all my life!" Alice said as she walked in the woods. Just as she said this, she noticed that one of the trees had a door leading right into it. "That's very curious!" she thought. "I think I may as well go in." And in she went.

Once more she found herself in the long hall and close to the little glass table. Taking the little golden key, she unlocked the door that led into the garden. She then ate the mushroom till she was about a foot high, and walked down the little passage. Finally she found herself in the beautiful garden, among the bright flowerbeds and the cool fountains.

Chapter 8

The Queen's Croquet Ground

There was a large rose tree at the garden's entrance. The roses growing on it were white, but there were three gardeners painting them red. Suddenly, they saw Alice approaching them.

"Excuse me, but why are you painting the roses red?" asked Alice.

The gardeners were 3 cards. They told Alice that this was supposed to be a red rose tree, but they planted a white rose tree instead. "If the queen finds out, she'll cut off our heads!" they added in a frightened whisper.

At that moment, one of the cards, who had been anxiously looking across the garden, called out, "The queen! The queen!" and the three gardeners instantly threw themselves flat upon their

faces. There was a sound of many footsteps, and Alice looked around, eager to see the queen.

First came ten card soldiers carrying clubs, with their hands and feet at the corners, then ten card courtiers ornamented all over with diamonds. After them came the ten royal children all ornamented with hearts.

Next came the guests, mostly kings and queens, and among them Alice recognized the White Rabbit. Then followed the Knave of Hearts, carrying the king's crown on a crimson velvet cushion; and at the end of this grand procession came the King and Queen of Hearts.

Alice was rather doubtful whether she ought not to lie down on her face like the three gardeners. But she could not remember ever having heard of such a rule at processions. "Besides, what would be the use of a procession," thought she, "if people had all to lie down upon their faces, so that they couldn't see it?"

So she stood still where she was, and waited. When the procession came to Alice, they all stopped and looked at her.

The queen saw Alice and asked severely, "Who is this?" She said it to the Knave of Hearts, who only bowed and smiled in reply. "Idiot!" said the queen, tossing her head impatiently and, turning to Alice, she went on: "What's your name, child?"

"My name is Alice, Your Majesty," said Alice very politely.

"And who are these?" said the queen, pointing to the three gardeners who were lying around the rose tree; for, you see, as they were lying on their faces, and the pattern on their backs was the same as the rest of the pack, she could not tell whether they were gardeners, or soldiers, or courtiers, or three of her own children.

"How should I know?" said Alice, surprised at her own courage. "It's no business of mine."

The queen turned crimson with fury and, after glaring at her for a moment like a wild beast, screamed, "Off with her head! Off—"

"Nonsense!" said Alice, very loudly and decidedly, and the queen was silent. The king laid his hand upon her arm and timidly said, "Consider, my dear, that she is only a child!"

The queen turned angrily away from him and said to the knave, "Turn them over!" The knave did so, very carefully, with one foot. "Get up!" said the queen, in a shrill, loud voice, and the three gardeners instantly jumped up. "What have you been doing here?"

"Please, Your Majesty," said one of the cards, in a very humble tone. "We were trying—"

"I see!" said the queen, who had been examining the roses. "Off with their heads!" And the procession moved on, three of the soldiers remaining behind to execute the unfortunate gardeners, who ran to Alice for protection. She put them into a large flowerpot that stood near her. The three soldiers wandered about for a minute or two, looking for them, and then quietly marched off after the others. "Are their heads off?" shouted the queen.

"Their heads are gone, if it pleases Your Majesty!" the soldiers shouted in reply.

Grunting in reply, the queen turned to Alice. "Can you play croquet?" she shouted.

"Yes!" said Alice loudly.

"Come on, then!" roared the queen, and Alice joined the procession, wondering very much what would happen next.

"Fine day, isn't it!" said a timid voice to Alice. She was walking by the White Rabbit, who was peeping anxiously into her face.

"Very," said Alice. "Where's the duchess?"

"Hush!" said the Rabbit in

a low, hurried tone. He looked anxiously over his shoulder as he spoke, and then raised himself up on tiptoe, put his mouth close to her ear, and whispered, "She is sentenced to be executed!"

"What? But why?" asked Alice, shocked.

"She boxed the queen's ears," the Rabbit said.

Alice gave a little scream of laughter. "Quiet!" the Rabbit whispered in a frightened tone.

"The queen will hear you! You see, she came rather late, and the queen said—"

"Get to your places!" shouted the queen in a voice of thunder, and everyone began running about in all directions, tumbling up against one another. They got settled down in a minute or two, and the game began.

Alice had never seen such a curious croquet ground in her life; it was all ridges and furrows. The croquet balls were live hedgehogs, and the mallets were live flamingos. The soldiers had to double themselves

up and stand on their hands and feet, to make the arches.

The main difficulty for Alice at first was managing her flamingo; she succeeded in getting its body tucked away, comfortably enough, under her arm, with its legs hanging down. But just as she had got its neck nicely straightened out and was going to give the hedgehog a blow with its head, it would twist itself around and look up in her face with such a puzzled expression that she could not help from bursting out laughing. And when she had got its head down, and was going to begin again, it was very provoking to find that the hedgehog had unrolled itself, and was in the act of crawling away. Besides all this, there was generally a ridge or furrow in the way wherever she wanted to send the hedgehog to, The doubled-up soldiers were always getting up and walking off to other parts of the ground, Alice soon came to the conclusion that it was a very difficult game indeed.

The players all played at once, without waiting for turns, quarreling all the while and fighting for the hedgehogs.

In a very short time the queen was in a furious passion and went stamping about and shouting, "Off with his head!" or "Off with her head!" about once every a minute. Alice began to feel very uneasy. To be sure, she had not as yet had any dispute with the queen, but she knew that it might happen any minute, "And then," thought she, "what would become of me? They're dreadfully fond of beheading people here. It's a wonder that there's anyone left alive!"

She looked around for a way to escape and wondered whether she could get away without being seen, when she noticed a curious appearance in the air. It puzzled her very much at first, but after watching it a minute or two, she made it out to be a grin, then she saw the Cheshire Cat's face appear in the air.

"How are you getting on?" asked the cat.

In another minute the whole

head appeared, and then Alice put down her flamingo and began an account of the game, feeling very glad she had someone to listen to her. The Cheshire Cat seemed to think that there was enough of itself now in sight, and did not make the rest of its body appear.

"I don't think they are playing

fair at all," complained Alice. "They fight with one another so much that you can't hear yourself speak. They don't have rules, either. If there are, nobody attends to them and you've no idea how confusing it is that all the things are alive. For instance, there's the arch I've got to go through next, walking about at the other end of the ground, and I should have croqueted the queen's hedgehog just now, only it ran away when it saw mine coming!"

"How do you like the queen?" asked the cat in a low voice.

"Not at all," said Alice. "She's so extremely—" Just then, she noticed that the queen was listening close behind her, so she went on—"likely to win that it's hardly worthwhile finishing the game."

The queen smiled and passed on.

"Who are you talking to?" asked the king, going up to Alice and looking at the cat's head with great curiosity.

"It's a friend of mine—a Cheshire Cat," said Alice. "Allow me to introduce it."

"I don't like the look of it at all," said the king. "However, it may kiss my hand, if it likes."

"I'd rather not," the cat remarked.

"Don't be impertinent," said the king, "and don't look at me like that!" He got behind Alice as he spoke. "It must be removed," he said very decidedly, and he called the queen, who was passing at the moment. "My dear! I wish you would have this cat removed!"

The queen had only one way of settling all difficulties, great or small. "Off with his head!" she said, without even looking round.

"I'll fetch the executioner myself," the king said eagerly, and he hurried off.

Alice thought she might as well go back and see how the game was going on. She heard the queen's voice in the distance, screaming with passion. She had already heard her sentence three of the players to be executed for having missed their turn, and she did not like the look of things at all. The game was in such confusion that she never knew whether it was her turn or not.

She went off in search of her hedgehog. The hedgehog was engaged in a fight with another hedgehog, and Alice thought this to be a good chance for croqueting one of them with the other. The only difficulty was that her flamingo was on the other side of the garden, helplessly trying to fly up into a tree.

By the time she had caught the flamingo and brought it back, the fight was over and both the hedgehogs were out of sight. "But it doesn't matter much," thought Alice, "as all the arches are gone from this side of the

ground." She caught the flamingo and tucked it away under her arm so that it might not escape again.

When she looked up again, she saw a large crowd gathered around the Cheshire Cat. There was a large dispute between the executioner, the queen, and the king over it. While they spoke all at once, the others just stood there looking uncomfortable.

The moment Alice appeared, they ran to her to tell her their side of the story. They begged her to solve the issue. But Alice found it hard to understand what any of them were saying as they all spoke together.

According to the executioner, a head can only be cut off if it is attached to a body. He clearly stated that he had never chopped off a body-less head in his life and he wasn't going to go about it now! The king said that anything having a head can be executed. As per the queen, she said that she'd have everyone executed if something wasn't done soon.

Having no proper reply, Alice replied diplomatically, "Since the cat belongs to the duchess, I think you should ask her about all this." The queen sent the executioner to fetch the duchess from the prison.

The moment the executioner left, the cat's head began to fade. It completely disappeared by the time he returned with the duchess. The king and the executioner ran all over the place looking for it, and the others got back to the game.

Chapter 9

The Mock Turtle's Story

Alice met the duchess, who had been set free. The duchess tucked her arm affectionately into Alice's, and they walked off together.

"You can't imagine how glad I am to see you, dear," said the

117

duchess. Alice was happy to find her in such a good mood and thought that maybe it was the pepper that had made her rude in the kitchen.

She thought to herself that if she were duchess, she'd make sure there was no pepper in the kitchen to make people hot-tempered, or vinegar to make them sour—maybe only sugar to make them sweet. "You're thinking about something, and that makes you forget to talk,

dear," said the duchess in her ear. "I can't tell you just now what the moral of that is, but I shall remember it in a bit."

"Perhaps it hasn't one," Alice remarked.

"Tut, tut, child!" said the duchess. "Everything's got a moral, if only you can find it." She squeezed herself close to Alice, making Alice feel very uncomfortable. The reason for this was that the duchess was quite ugly, and also because she was resting her very sharp chin on Alice's shoulder.

Alice could not be rude, so she decided to bear with it. She tried to keep the conversation going. "The game's going well now."

"So it is," said the duchess, "and the moral of that is—it's love that makes the world go around."

"Somebody said that it's done by everyone minding their own business," whispered Alice.

"It all means the same, and the moral of that is—take care of the sense, and the sounds will take care of themselves," the duchess said.

Alice thought of how fond the duchess was of finding morals. The duchess turned to her. "Are you wondering why my arm isn't around your waist? The reason is that I'm not sure if your flamingo is friendly or not. May I pet him?"

"He may bite," Alice cautioned her, holding the poor, squirming bird against her. She did not want the duchess to take this risk. The duchess agreed, saying that flamingos and mustard both bite. "The moral of that is—birds of a feather flock together."

"Mustard isn't a bird. It's a mineral, I think," pointed out Alice.

"Of course it is," the duchess said. "There's a large mustard mine over here. The moral of that is—the more there is of mine, the less there is of yours."

"I think I'd understand it better if you wrote it down. I can't quite follow it as you say it," Alice said politely. Then she fell quiet.

After a minute, the duchess looked at her. "Thinking again, my dear?" she asked, with a sharp dig of her pointed chin.

"I think I have the right to think," said Alice, a little annoyed.

The duchess continued: "Just about as much right as pigs have to fly, and the moral . . ."

To Alice's great surprise, the duchess's voice died away, and the arm that was linked into hers began to tremble. Alice looked up, and there stood the queen in front of them, with her arms folded, frowning!

"Good-good d-day, Your Ma-Majesty," the duchess stammered.

"I will give you a fair choice," shouted the queen. "Either you or you must have your head chopped off. Take your pick!"

The duchess made her choice and disappeared.

"Shall we get back to the game?" the queen asked Alice. Alice, who was too afraid to say anything, agreed. All through the game the queen never stopped quarreling and shouting, "Off with his head!" or, "Off with her head!" By the end of half an hour all the players, except the

king, the queen, and Alice, were facing execution.

The queen, quite out of breath, turned to Alice. "Have you seen the Mock Turtle yet?"

"No, I haven't," replied Alice. "I don't even know what a Mock Turtle is!"

"Come then," said the Queen. "I want you to meet him. He'll tell you the story of his life."

As they walked off together, Alice heard the king whisper to the crowd, "You are all pardoned." She was quite relieved. After walking with the queen for a long time, they saw came across a gryphon, fast asleep in the sun.

The gryphon is a creature with the head, wings, claws of an eagle and the body of a lion, tail included. Many believe the gryphon stands for the two qualities of the eagle and lion combined: courage and watchfulness.

The queen, of course, was unlike many. "Get up, lazy bones," she ordered the creature. "Take this young lady to the Mock Turtle so that she can hear his story. I must go back and see to the execution." Saying this, she walked off, leaving Alice alone with the gryphon. She did not quite like the way it looked. But she figured that it was much

safer than the queen. So she sat down and waited.

The gryphon woke up, rubbed its eyes, and watched the queen until she was far away from them. "What fun," it chuckled.

"Beg your pardon?" asked Alice.

"It's all her imagination. They never execute anybody. Come on." Alice thought she had never been ordered around so much in her life.

They hadn't gone far when they saw the Mock Turtle sitting sadly on a rock. She heard him sigh like his heart was breaking. "Why is he unhappy?" she asked the gryphon. It replied like before, that it was just his imagination. "He's not really unhappy. Come on."

They walked up to him. When he saw them, his eyes were full of tears. But he didn't say a word. The gryphon started: "This young lady wants to know the story of your life."

"I'll tell her," said the Mock Turtle. "Sit down, but don't say a word till I've finished."

They sat down. Alice waited patiently, holding her hands on her lap like a lady would. At last, with a deep sigh, the

Mock Turtle began. "Once, I was a real turtle." This was followed by a long stretch of silence, interrupted only by the guttural sound from the gryphon, or the Mock Turtle's sobbing.

Alice was about to thank him for an interesting story and leave, when he started again, "When we were little, we went to school in the sea." He was calmer now. "The teacher was an old turtle. We called him Tortoise."

"Why would you call him Tortoise?" asked Alice.

"Because he taught us to!" snapped the Mock Turtle.

The gryphon added, "You should be ashamed of yourself, asking something simple like that." They both stared at Alice until she felt like sinking into the earth. The gryphon urged the Mock Turtle to go on.

"Yes, where was I? Oh yes, we went to school in the sea. We had the best education. In fact, we went to school every day."

"I went to a day school, too," said Alice. "No need to be so proud of that."

"Were there extras?" asked the Mock Turtle anxiously.

"Yes, we learned French and

music," replied Alice.

"And washing?" inquired the Mock Turtle.

"Of course not," said Alice indignantly.

"Then yours wasn't a good school," said the Mock Turtle in a huff.

"Why would you want to learn washing? Especially not if you live at the bottom of the sea," said Alice.

"Unfortunately, I couldn't afford it. I only took the regular courses," said the Mock Turtle with a sigh. "Reeling, Writhing, different branches of Arithmetic— Ambition, Distraction, Uglification, and Derision."

"I've never heard of Uglification," murmured Alice, very confused.

"What is it?"

Hearing this, the gryphon threw up its paws in surprise. "Never heard of uglifying? I hope you know what to beautify is."

"Yes," said Alice. "It means to make anything prettier."

"Well, if you don't know what uglifying is, then you are a simpleton," said the gryphon.

Alice shook her head and turned to the Mock Turtle. "What else did you learn?"

"Well, there was Mystery," he said, counting off the subjects on his flappers, "Ancient and Modern, Seaography, Drawling and Stretching, Fainting with Coils."

"What was that like?" inquired Alice.

"Can't show you. I'm too stiff,"

said the Mock Turtle. "Gryphon here never learned it."

"Never had the time. I went to the Classics teacher, though. Old crab, he was," the gryphon said.

"How many hours a day did you spend in school?" asked Alice.

"First day, ten hours," replied the Mock Turtle. "Nine the next, and so on."

"What a curious plan," thought Alice.

"That's why they are called lessons, for they lessen each day," said the gryphon. "Then day eleven must have been a holiday," said Alice.

The Mock Turtle agreed. "How did you manage the twelfth day?" she asked.

"Enough about lessons," said the gryphon. "Tell her something about the games."

Chapter 10

The Lobster Quadrille

The Mock Turtle sighed deeply, looked sadly at Alice, and tried to speak. His voice choked once or twice. The gryphon started thumping his friend on the back, explaining that he probably had a bone stuck in his throat.

Recovered at last, the Mock Turtle said, "You may not have

lived much under the sea."

"I haven't," agreed Alice.

"Perhaps you were never introduced to a lobster."

Alice was about to say that she

had tasted one but denied knowing a lobster. "You have no idea how delightful a lobster quadrille can be," said the Mock Turtle. "Well, you just be patient. I'll tell you all about it."

Alice replied eagerly, "Oh, I know it is a dance of sort, but I don't know how it goes."

"It is a square dance," said the gryphon, jumping in front of her. "First you form a line along the seashore—"

"Two lines!" cried the Mock Turtle, who did not want to be ignored. "Seals, turtles, salmon, etc. When you've cleaned the jellyfish out of the way, you advance twice."

"Each time with a lobster

as your partner," added the gryphon.

"Of course," the Mock Turtle said. "Advance twice, set to partners—"

"—change lobsters, and retire in same order," continued the gryphon.

"Then, you know," the Mock Turtle went on, "you throw the—"

"The lobsters!" shouted the gryphon, with a bound into the air.

"—as far out to sea as you can—"

"Swim after them!" screamed the gryphon.

"Turn a somersault in the sea!" cried the Mock Turtle, capering wildly about.

"Change lobsters again!" yelled the gryphon at the top of its voice.

"Back to land again, and that's all the first figure," said the Mock Turtle, suddenly dropping his voice; and the two creatures, who had been jumping about like mad things all this time sat down again very sadly and quietly and looked at Alice.

"It must be a very pretty dance," said Alice timidly.

"Would you like to see a little of it?" said the Mock Turtle.

"Very much indeed," said Alice.

"Come, let's try the first figure!" said the Mock Turtle to the gryphon. "We can do without lobsters, you know. Who shall sing?"

"Oh, you sing," said the gryphon. "I've forgotten the words."

So they began solemnly dancing around and around Alice, every now and then treading on her toes when they passed too close, and waving their forepaws to mark the time while the Mock

Turtle sang this, very slowly and sadly:

"Will you walk a little faster?" said a whiting to a snail.

"There's a porpoise close behind us, and he's treading on my tail. See how eagerly the lobsters and the turtles all advance!"

"They are waiting on the shingle— will you come and join the dance?"

"Will you, won't you, will you, won't you, will you join the dance?"

"Will you, won't you, will you, won't you, won't you join the dance?"

"You can really have no notion how delightful it will be."

"When they take us up and throw us, with the lobsters, out to sea!"

"But the snail replied, 'Too far,

too far!' and gave a look askance—"

"Said he thanked the whiting kindly, but he would not join the dance."

"Would not, could not, would not, could not, would not join the dance."

"Would not, could not, would not, could not, could not join the dance."

"'What matters it how far we go?' his scaly friend replied."

"'There is another shore, you know, upon the other side.'"

"The further off from England, the nearer it is to France—"

"Then turn not pale, beloved snail, but come and join the dance."

"Will you, won't you, will you, won't

you, will you join the dance?"

"Will you, won't you, will you, won't you, won't you join the dance?"

"Thank you, it's a very interesting dance to watch," said Alice, feeling very glad that it was over at last, "and I do so like that curious song about the whiting!"

"Oh, as to the whiting," said the Mock Turtle, "they—you've seen them, of course?"

"Yes," said Alice, "I've often seen them at dinn—" She checked herself hastily.

"I don't know where Dinn may be," said the Mock Turtle, "but if you've seen them so often, of course you know what they're like."

"I believe so," Alice replied

thoughtfully. "They have their tails in their mouths—and they're all over crumbs."

"You're wrong about the crumbs," said the Mock Turtle, "crumbs would all wash off in the sea. But they have their tails in their mouths; and the reason is—" Here, the Mock Turtle yawned and shut his eyes. "Tell her about the reason and all that," he said to the gryphon.

"The reason is," said the gryphon, "that they would go with the lobsters to the dance. So they got thrown out to sea. So they had to fall a long way. So they got their tails tuck in their mouths. And they couldn't get them out again. That's all."

"Thank you," said Alice, "it's very interesting. I never knew so much about a whiting before."

"I can tell you more than that, if you like," said the gryphon. "Do you know why it's called a whiting?"

"I never thought about it," said Alice. "Why?"

"It does the boots and shoes," the gryphon replied very solemnly.

Alice was thoroughly puzzled. "Does the boots and shoes!" she repeated in a wondering tone.

"What are your shoes done with?" said the gryphon. "I mean, what makes them so shiny?"

Alice looked down at them and thought a little before she gave her answer. "They're done with blacking,

I believe."

"Boots and shoes under the sea," the gryphon went on in a deep voice, "are done with a whiting. Now you know."

"And what are they made of?" Alice asked in a tone of great curiosity. "Soles and eels, of course," the gryphon replied rather impatiently. "Any shrimp could have told you that."

"If I'd been the whiting," said Alice, whose thoughts were still running on the song, "I'd have said to the porpoise, "Keep back, please. We don't want you with us!"

"They were obliged to have him with them," the Mock Turtle said. "No wise fish would go anywhere without a porpoise. If a fish came to me and told me he was going a journey, I would say, 'With what porpoise?'"

"Don't you mean 'purpose'?" said Alice.

"I mean what I say," the Mock Turtle replied in an offended tone.

And the gryphon added, "Come, let's hear some of your adventures."

"I could tell you my adventures—beginning from this morning," said Alice a little timidly, "but it's no use going back to yesterday, because I was a different person then."

"Explain all that," said the Mock Turtle.

"No, no! The adventures first," said the gryphon in an impatient tone. "Explanations take such a dreadful lot of time."

So Alice began telling them her adventures from the time when she first saw the White Rabbit. She was a little nervous about it at first, as the two creatures got so close to her, one on each side, and opened their eyes and mouths so

very wide, but she gained courage as she went on.

"It's all about as curious as it can be," said the gryphon. "Stand up and repeat."

Her head was so full of the Lobster quadrille that she hardly knew what she was saying, and the words came very queer indeed:

"Tis the voice of the Lobster"
I heard him declare,
"You have baked me too brown, I must sugar my hair."
As a duck with its eyelids, so he with his nose.
Trims his belt and his buttons, and turns out his toes.
When the sands are all dry, he is gay as a lark,
And will talk in contemptuous

tones of the shark,
But, when the tide rises and
sharks are around,
His voice has a timid and
tremulous sound.

"Well, I never heard it before!" exclaimed the Mock Turtle. "But it sounds like utter rubbish.

Alice said nothing. She had sat down with her face in her hands, wondering if anything would ever happen in a natural way again.

"I think you should stop now," said the gryphon, and Alice was only too glad to do so.

"Shall we try another figure of the lobster quadrille?" the gryphon went on. "Or would you like the Mock Turtle to sing you a song?"

"Oh, a song would be lovely,

if the Mock Turtle wouldn't mind," said Alice.

"Sing her 'Turtle Soup' will you, old fellow?" said the Gryphon.

The Mock Turtle sighed deeply, and began, in a voice sometimes choked with sobs, to sing this:

Beautiful Soup, so rich and green,
Waiting in a hot tureen!
Who for such dainties would not stoop?
Soup of the evening, beautiful Soup!
Soup of the evening, beautiful Soup!
Beau—ootiful Soo—oop!
Beau—ootiful Soo—oop!
Soo—oop of the e—e—evening,
Beautiful, beautiful Soup!
Beautiful Soup! Who cares for fish,

Game, or any other dish?

Who would not give all else for two Pennyworth only of beautiful Soup?

Pennyworth only of beautiful Soup?

Beau—ootiful Soo—oop!

Beau—ootiful Soo—oop!

Soo—oop of the e—e—evening,

Beautiful, beauti—FUL SOUP!

As the Mock Turtle continued singing, a cry was heard in the distance. "The trial's beginning!" The gryphon caught Alice's hand and started to pull her, "Come on!"

As she rushed off with the gryphon, Alice could hear the words becoming fainter,

Soo—oop of the e—e—evening,

Beautiful, beautiful Soup!

Chapter 11

Who Stole the Tarts?

The King and Queen of Hearts were seated on their throne when they arrived, and a great crowd assembled about them—all sorts of little birds and beasts, as well as the whole pack of cards. The knave was standing before them, in chains, with a soldier on each

side to guard him, and near the king was the White Rabbit, with a trumpet in one hand and a scroll of parchment in the other.

In the very middle of the court was a table with a large dish of tarts upon it: They looked so good that it made Alice quite hungry to look at them. "I wish they'd get the trial done," she thought, "and hand around the refreshments!" But there seemed to be no chance of this, so she began looking at everything about her, to pass away the time.

Alice had never been in a court of justice before, but she had read about them in books and was quite pleased to find that she knew the name of nearly everything there. "That's the judge," she said to herself, "because of his great wig."

The judge was the king and he wore his crown over his great wig. "And that's the jury-box," thought Alice, "and those twelve creatures" (she was obliged to say "creatures," you see, because some of them were animals, and some were birds), I suppose they are the jurors." She said these last word two or three times over to herself, being rather proud of it for she thought that very few little girls of her age knew the meaning of it at all. However, "jury-men" would have done just as well.

The twelve jurors were all

writing very busily on slates. "What are they doing?" Alice whispered to the gryphon. "They can't have anything to put down yet, before the trial's begun."

"They're putting down their names," the gryphon whispered in reply, "for fear they should forget them before the end of the trial."

"Stupid things!" Alice began in a loud, indignant voice, but she stopped hastily, for just then, the

White Rabbit cried out, "Silence in the court!"

Alice could see as well as if she were looking over their shoulders, that all the jurors were writing down "stupid things!" on their slates, and she could even make out that one of them didn't know how to spell "stupid."

One of the jurors had a pencil that squeaked. This, of course, Alice could not stand, and she went around the court, got behind him, and very soon found an opportunity to take it away. She did it so quickly that the poor little juror could not make out at all what had become of it. So, after hunting all about for it, he was obliged to write with one finger for the rest of the day. This was of very little use, as it left no mark on the slate.

"Read the accusation!" said the king.

The White Rabbit blew three blasts on the trumpet, then unrolled the parchment-scroll and read:

"The Queen of Hearts, she made some tarts, all on a summer day; The Knave of Hearts, he stole those tarts, and took them quite away!"

"Consider your verdict," the king said to the jury.

"Not yet, not yet!" the Rabbit hastily interrupted. "There's a great deal to come before that!"

"Call the first witness," said

the king; and the White Rabbit blew three blasts on the trumpet and called out, "First witness!" It was the Hatter. He came in with a teacup in one hand and a piece of bread and butter in the other. "I beg pardon, Your Majesty," he began, "for bringing these in, but I hadn't quite finished my tea when I was sent for."

"You should have finished," said the king. "When did you begin?" The Mad Hatter looked at the March Hare, who had followed him into the court, arm in arm with the dormouse. "Fourteenth of March, I think," he said.

"Fifteenth," said the March Hare.

"Sixteenth," added the

dormouse.

"Write that down," the king said to the jury, and the jury eagerly wrote down all three dates on their slates. "Take off your hat," the king said to the Hatter.

"It isn't mine," said the Hatter.

"Stolen!" the king exclaimed, turning to the jury, who instantly made a note of the fact.

"I keep them to sell," the Hatter added as an explanation. "I've none of my own. I'm a hatter."

Here, the queen put on her spectacles and began staring at the Hatter, who turned pale and fidgeted.

"Give your evidence," said the king, "and don't be nervous, or I'll have you executed on the spot." This did not seem to encourage the witness at all—he kept shifting from one foot to the other, looking uneasily at the queen, and in his confusion, the Hatter bit a large piece out of his teacup instead of the bread and butter.

Just at this moment, Alice felt a very curious sensation, which puzzled her a good deal until she made out what it was. She was beginning to grow again! She thought at first she would get up and leave the court; but on second thought, she decided to remain where she was as long as there was room for her.

"I wish you wouldn't squeeze so," said the dormouse, who was sitting next to her. "I can hardly breathe."

"I can't help it," said Alice very meekly. "I'm growing."

"You've no right to grow here," said the dormouse.

"Don't talk nonsense," said Alice more boldly. "You know you're growing, too."

"Yes, but I grow at a reasonable pace," said the dormouse, "not in that ridiculous fashion." And he got up very sulkily and crossed over to the other side of the court.

All this time the queen had never left off staring at the Hatter, and just as the dormouse crossed the court, she said to one of the officers of the court, "Bring me the list of the singers in the last concert!" on which the wretched Hatter trembled so, that he shook both his shoes off.

"Give your evidence," the king repeated angrily, "or I'll have you executed, whether you're nervous or not."

"I'm a poor man, Your Majesty," the Hatter began, in a trembling voice, "and I hadn't begun my tea— not above a week or so—and what with the bread and butter getting so thin—and the twinkling of the tea—"

"The twinkling of the what?" asked the king.

"It began with the tea," the Hatter replied.

"Of course twinkling begins with a T!" said the king sharply. "Do you take me for a dunce? Go on!"

"I'm a poor man," the Hatter

went on, "and most things twinkled after that—only the March Hare said—"

"I didn't!" the March Hare

interrupted in a great hurry.

"You did!" said the Hatter.

"I deny it!" said the March Hare.

"He denies it," said the king, "Leave out that part."

"Well, at any rate, the Dormouse said," the Hatter went on, looking anxiously around to see if he would deny it, too. But the Dormouse denied nothing, being fast asleep.

"After that," continued the Hatter, "I cut some more bread and butter—"

"But what did the dormouse say?" one of the jury asked.

"That, I can't remember," said the Hatter.

"You must remember," remarked the king, "or I'll have

you executed."

The miserable Hatter dropped his teacup and bread and butter, and went down on one knee. "I'm a poor man, Your Majesty," he began.

"You're a very poor speaker," said the king. "You may go." The Mad Hatter hurriedly left the court without even waiting to put his shoes on.

"—and just take his head off outside," the queen added to one of the officers, but the Hatter was out of sight before the officer could get to the door.

"Call the next witness!" said the king.

It was the cook. She carried the pepper-box in her hand

and the people near the door
began sneezing.

"Give your evidence," said
the king.

"Won't," said the cook.

The king looked anxiously at

the White Rabbit, who said, in a low voice, "Your Majesty must cross-examine this witness."

"Well, if I must, I must," the king said, with a melancholy air, and after folding his arms and frowning at the cook till his eyes were nearly out of sight, he said in a deep voice, "What are tarts made of?"

"Pepper, mostly," said the cook.

"Treacle," said a sleepy voice behind her.

"Collar that dormouse," the queen shrieked out. "Behead that dormouse! Turn that dormouse out of court! Suppress him! Pinch him! Off with his whiskers!"

For some minutes the whole court was in confusion, getting the dormouse turned out. By the time they had settled down again, the cook had disappeared.

"Never mind!" said the king, "call the next witness." And he added in an undertone to the queen, "Really, my dear, must you cross-examine the next witness? It quite makes my forehead ache!"

Alice watched the White Rabbit as he fumbled over the list. Imagine her surprise when he called out in his shrill little voice, "Alice!"

Chapter 12

Alice's Evidence

"Here!" cried Alice, quite forgetting in the flurry of the moment how large she had grown in the last few minutes. She jumped up in such a hurry that she tipped over the jury-box with the edge of her skirt, upsetting all the jury-men onto the

heads of the crowd below, and there
they lay sprawling about.

"Oh, I beg your pardon!" she
exclaimed, and began picking them
up again as quickly as she could.

"The trial cannot proceed," said the king in a very grave voice, "until all the jurymen are back in their proper places. . . . All," he repeated with great emphasis, looking hard at Alice as he said so.

As soon as the jury had recovered a little from the shock of being upset, and their slates and pencils had been found and handed back to them, they set to work very diligently to write out a history of the accident;

"What do you know about this business?" the king said to Alice.

"Nothing whatsoever," said Alice.

"That's very important," the king said, turning to the jury.

They were just beginning to

write this down on their slates, when the White Rabbit interrupted, "Unimportant, Your Majesty means, of course," he said in a very respectful tone, but frowning and making faces at him as he spoke.

"Unimportant, of course, is what I meant," the king hastily said;

Some of the jury wrote it down "important," and some "unimportant." Alice could see this, as she was near enough to look over their slates.

At this moment the king, who had been for some time busily writing in his notebook, cackled out, "Silence!" and read out from his book, "Rule 42: ALL PERSONS MORE THAN

A MILE HIGH TO LEAVE THE COURT."

"I'm not a mile high," said Alice.

"You are," said the king.

"Nearly two miles high," said the queen.

"Well, I shan't go, at any rate," said Alice. "Besides, that's not a regular rule—you invented it just now."

"It's the oldest rule in the book," said the king.

"Then it ought to be number one," said Alice.

The King turned pale and shut his notebook hastily. "Consider your verdict," he said to the jury, in a low, trembling voice.

"Your Majesty, we still have

more evidence," said the White Rabbit. He unfolded the paper as he spoke and added, "It's a set of verses. It seems to be written by the prisoner to somebody."

"Who is it directed to?" asked one of the jurymen.

"It isn't directed at all," said the White Rabbit. "In fact, there's nothing written on the outside." He unfolded the paper as he spoke, and added, "It isn't a letter, after all. It's a set of verses."

"Are they in the prisoner's handwriting?" asked another of the jurymen.

"No, they're not," said the White Rabbit, "and that's the queerest thing about it." The jury all looked puzzled.

"He must have imitated somebody else's hand," said the king. The jury all brightened up again.

"Please, Your Majesty," said the knave. "I didn't write it, and they can't prove that I did. There's no name signed at the end."

"If you didn't sign it," said the king, "that only makes the matter worse. You must have meant some mischief, or else you'd have signed your name like an honest man."

There was a general clapping of hands at this—it was the first really clever thing the king had said that day.

"That proves his guilt," said the queen.

"It proves nothing of the sort!" said Alice. "Why, you don't even know what it's about!"

The king ordered the Rabbit to read it. These were the verses the White Rabbit read:

'They told me you had
been to her,
And mentioned me to him:
She gave me a good character,
But said I could not swim.
He sent them word I had not gone
(We know it to be true):
If she should push the matter on,
What would become of you?
I gave her one, they gave him two,
You gave us three or more;
They all returned from him to you,
Though they were mine before.
If I or she should chance to be

Involved in this affair,
He trusts to you to set them free,
Exactly as we were.
My notion was that you had been
(Before she had this fit)
An obstacle that came between
Him, and ourselves, and it.
Don't let him know she liked
them best,
For this must ever be
A secret, kept from all the rest,
Between yourself and me.'

"That's the most important piece of evidence we've heard yet," said the king after hearing it.

"If any one of them can explain it," said Alice, "I don't believe there's an atom of meaning in it." She had grown so large in the last few minutes that she wasn't a bit afraid of interrupting him.

"All right, so far," said the king, and he went on muttering over the verses to himself: "WE KNOW IT TO BE TRUE—that's the jury, of course. "I GAVE HER ONE, THEY GAVE HIM TWO—why, that must be what he did with the tarts, you know—"

"But, it goes on—THEY ALL RETURNED FROM HIM TO YOU," said Alice.

"Why, there they are!" said the king triumphantly, pointing to the tarts on the table. "Nothing can be clearer than that."

Then again—"BEFORE SHE HAD THIS FIT—you've never had fits, my dear, I think?" he said to the queen.

"Never!" said the queen furiously.

"Then the words don't fit you," said the king, looking around the court with a smile. There was dead silence.

"If there's no meaning in it," said the king, "let the jury consider their verdict."

"No, no!" said the queen. "Sentence first—verdict afterward."

"What nonsense!" said Alice loudly. "The idea of having the sentence first!"

"Silence!" roared the queen, turning purple with anger.

"I won't!" said Alice.

"Off with her head!" the queen shouted at the top of her voice. Nobody moved.

"Who cares for you?" said Alice. She had grown to her full size by this time. "You're nothing but a pack of cards!"

At this, the whole pack rose up in the air and came down upon her. She gave a little scream and tried to beat them off.

All of a sudden, Alice found

herself lying on the bank, with her head in her sister's lap, who was gently brushing away some dead leaves that had fluttered down from the trees upon her face.

"Wake up, Alice dear!" said her sister. "Why, what a long sleep you've had!"

"Oh, I've had such a curious

dream!" said Alice, and she told her sister all the strange adventures as well as she could remember. When she had finished, her sister kissed her and said, "It was a curious dream, dear, certainly. But now run in for your tea; it's getting late." So Alice got up and ran off, thinking while she ran, as well she might, what a wonderful dream it had been.

But her sister sat still just as she left her, thinking of little Alice and all her wonderful adventures, till she too began dreaming. This was her dream:

First, she dreamed of little Alice. The whole place around her became alive, with the strange creatures of her little sister's dream.

The long grass rustled at her feet as the White Rabbit hurried

by, the mouse splashing away; she could hear the rattle of the teacups as the March Hare and his friends shared their never-ending meal, and the shrill voice of the queen.

Once more the pig-baby was sneezing on the duchess' knee.

So she sat on, with closed eyes, and half believed herself in Wonderland. Though she knew she had but to open her eyes again and all would change to dull reality.

The grass would be only rustling in the wind, and the pool rippling to the waving of the reeds, the rattling teacups would change to tinkling sheep-bells, and the queen's shrill cries to the voice of the shepherd boy. The sneeze of the baby, the shriek of the gryphon, and all the other queer noises would change, she knew, to the confused clamor of the busy farmyard, while the mowing of the cattle in the distance would

take the place of the Mock Turtle's heavy sobs.

Lastly, she pictured to herself how this same little sister of hers would, in the after-time, be herself a grown woman, and how she would keep, through all her riper years, the simple and loving heart of her childhood. How she would gather about her other little children, and make their eyes bright and eager with many a strange tale, perhaps even with the dream of Wonderland of long ago.

About the Author

Charles Dodgson (January 27, 1832 - January 14, 1898) grew up in a Church family. He was a brilliant mathematician, but he was more interested in writing imaginative stories. When he started writing, he changed his name to Lewis Carroll.

Lewis Carroll was a great entertainer and a genius at story-telling. His famous Alice stories were created in 1862, when he had gone for an outing with three young children of his close friend. One of the children called Alice Liddell, after whom the famous Alice is named, forced him to write this story which made him famous.

The Adventures of Tom Sawyer
The Adventures of Pinocchio
Alice in Wonderland
Anne of Green Gables
Beauty and the Beast
Black Beauty
The Call of the Wild
A Christmas Carol
Frankenstein
Great Expectations
Journey to the Center of the Earth
The Jungle Book
King Arthur and the Knights of the Round Table
Little Women
Moby Dick
The Night Before Christmas and Other Holiday Tales
Oliver Twist
Peter Pan
The Prince and the Pauper
Pygmalion
The Secret Garden
The Time Machine
Treasure Island
White Fang
The Wind in the Willows
The Wizard of Oz